Heat the oven to 350 degrees. Lightly whip the eggs with a wire whisk until light-colored. Beat in the remaining sugar and gradually add the juices and rinds. Continue beating until you can't beat any longer. Then give exactly ten more strokes. Pour the mixture into the cups. Place the cups in a pan of shallow hot water and bake for 45 minutes, or until a knife inserted in the custard comes out clean. Remove the cups from the water and cool. Do not refrigerate.

To serve, flan may be unmolded onto dessert plates.

When I was little, an older brother convinced me that life is
just one wonderful story after another. Thanks, Gaddis.
—C. G.

To the Rio Café, best flan north of Mexico
—P. M.

Atheneum Books for Young Readers
An imprint of Simon & Schuster Children's Publishing Division
1230 Avenue of the Americas
New York, New York 10020

Book design by Ann Bobco
The text of this book is set in Centaur MT.
The illustrations are rendered in watercolor.

Printed in Hong Kong
10 9 8 7 6 5 4 3 2 1

Library of Congress Cataloging-in-Publication Data
Geeslin, Campbell.
How Nanita learned to make flan / by Campbell Geeslin ;
illustrated by Petra Mathers.
p. cm.
"An Anne Schwartz book."
Summary: The cobbler in a tiny Mexican town is so busy that he cannot make
shoes for his daughter, so she makes her own shoes, which take her far away
to a rich man's home where she must clean and cook all day. Includes a recipe
for flan.
ISBN 0-689-81546-8
[1. Shoes—Fiction. 2. Mexico—Fiction. 3. Cookery, Mexican—Fiction.]
I. Mathers, Petra, ill. II. Title.
PZ7.G25845Ho 1999
[E]—dc21
96-50154

FIRST
EDITION

How Nanita learned to make flan

by campbell geeslin

illustrated by

petra mathers

An Anne Schwartz Book

ATHENEUM BOOKS FOR YOUNG READERS

The Mexican town where Nanita lives

is too small to be found on any map.

Nanita's papa is the shoemaker. He makes boots for the colonel, shiny shoes for the mayor, red slippers for the dancing teacher, and black shoes for the priest.

Nanita likes to watch her papa cut and sew and tack the leather. *Tap, tap, tap* goes his little hammer. He works so hard that Nanita has never seen him smile. And because he is always busy, Nanita has no shoes of her own.

One day Nanita says to him, "Soon it will be my First Communion. I can't go before Our Lady of Guadalupe without shoes!"

Papa frowns and says, "Oh, I have too much work! I will try, I promise. But there is no time, no time."

Days go by, and Papa is still not able to make shoes for Nanita. But Nanita does not want to wait any longer, so she decides to make them for herself. She has watched him, so she knows how to do it, doesn't she?

That night, when Nanita hears Papa snoring, she slips down
the stairs into the shop.

"My feet are small," she says to herself. "I won't use much
leather." She traces around each foot for the soles, cuts them out
with Papa's sharp scissors, and punches forty-eight holes around
the edges, just the way she has seen him do. She cuts out tops
from scraps of red, yellow, blue, and green leather she finds on
the floor. Then she sews and tacks the leather — *tap, tap, tap* —
with Papa's little hammer.

When her shoes are finished,
Nanita slips them on and yawns.
They feel strange, of course, but
wonderful, too. She is so proud of
them that she wears them to bed.

During the night, the new shoes
become restless. They get out of bed
and go out into the dark.

The shoes walk
and walk . . . with
Nanita in them!

When Nanita wakes at dawn, she sees nothing but sand and a few dusty bushes. "Where am I?" she asks. She is thirsty and hot. "Oh," she says, "I don't like this place."

Far away, where the desert turns into purple mountains, Nanita sees a grand house. The shoes walk on, and when at last they get to the front door, she knocks timidly. A ranchero with a huge mustache appears. "What do you want?" he asks gruffly.

"Oh please, sir," Nanita says. "I am lost, and I am so thirsty and hungry!"

Just then an old woman comes to the door. The ranchero says to her, "Put this girl to work. After she has cleaned the house, give her a tortilla and some water, and let her sleep on the kitchen floor."

The old woman sees Nanita's shoes and her eyes grow big. "Oh, look at all the colors!" she exclaims. "Give me those!"

The old woman forces her big feet into Nanita's little shoes.

Now every morning the old woman kicks Nanita awake with the toe of one of Nanita's shoes. The old woman's feet hurt, so she makes Nanita gather sticks and light the oven and dust the furniture and scrub all the floors. Nanita wishes the shoes would walk the old lady far, far away, but they don't. Maybe it's because she's too big for them, Nanita thinks.

Nanita stomps her bare foot. "I'm just a little girl," she cries. "I can't do all the work!" But she can't go home because she doesn't know the way.

One day the ranchero brings home an old parrot with a patch over one eye. He chains the green-and-yellow bird to a perch in the dining room and says, "Now I have someone to entertain me at dinner. If you aren't funny, Señor Parrot, I'll have the old woman fry you for breakfast."

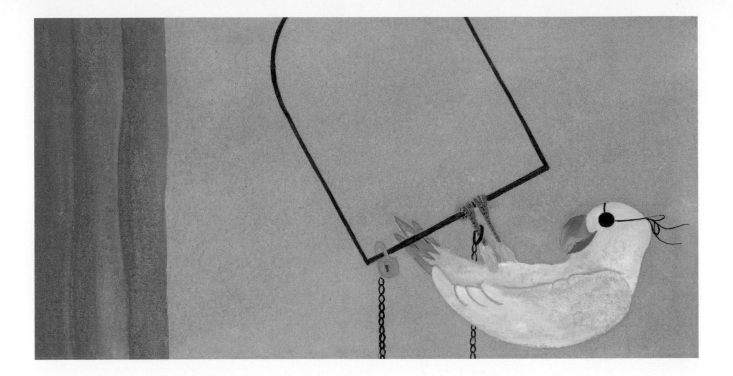

The next day, when Nanita is scrubbing the dining-room floor, Señor Parrot says to her, "Guess what I am?"

"Parrots talk, so you must be a parrot," she replies.

"No, no! Look at the way I'm hanging from my perch."

Nanita looks and then shakes her head. "I'm sorry," she says, "but you still look like a parrot to me."

"Can't you see the way I'm curved over? Green and yellow? Don't I remind you of a half-ripe banana?"

Nanita laughs and laughs, and she and Señor Parrot become friends. He tells stories about how he was kidnapped in the jungle, sold to a pirate captain, and ended up entertaining Queen Blanca of Spain.

When the old woman hears all their chatter, she screams at Nanita, "I see that you don't have enough work to do! Standing up to beat eggs makes my feet hurt. You will make flan for tonight's dessert." And she teaches Nanita how.

Nanita beats and beats the eggs. "Oh, my elbow is tired!" she groans.

Señor Parrot calls out, "Ten more! When you are so tired that you can't beat the eggs any longer, you must give them exactly ten more strokes."

Nanita sighs, but she does ten more strokes. Then she bakes the six cups of flan in a pan of steaming water.

That evening when the ranchero is served his dessert, he smacks his lips. "Old woman!" he roars. "This is the best flan I ever tasted! I want it every night."

So every day after Nanita builds a fire, scrubs the floors, and dusts the furniture, she must whisk eggs, sugar, orange and lemon juice to make flan. And every evening the ranchero sings happily to himself as he eats all six cups.

With each day Nanita grows wearier. Soon not even Señor Parrot can make her laugh. She thinks of her papa who works all the time.

No wonder he never smiles. He's too tired!

One morning as Nanita is dusting, Señor Parrot whispers, "My friend White Dove flew by yesterday and told me that your papa cries every day because you are gone. If you will free me, I'll show you the way back to him."

Nanita is astonished. "Poor Papa," she says. "I want to go home!"

Early the next morning Nanita tiptoes into the old woman's room and takes the shoes. She unchains Señor Parrot, and they set off.

Nanita and Señor Parrot cross the desert. When the shoes try to
go where they want, Nanita stomps.

At last Nanita and Señor Parrot get to her village.

"Oh, my little house is the most beautiful house in the world!" she cries as she runs toward it. "Papa! Papa!"

Her papa rushes out, weeping with joy. "Oh, Nanita, Nanita! Where have you been? I've missed you every minute!" he cries.

But then Papa sees her dusty, worn shoes. "Who gave you those?" he asks, scowling. "Take them off, and we'll make you a new pair today."

"*Cough! Cough!* This desert air must not be good for me. How I long to get back to my family in the jungle!" Señor Parrot says.

Nanita wishes he wouldn't leave, but she says, "I know what it's like to be homesick."

Papa thanks Señor Parrot and gives him a little gold chain to wear around his neck.

The big bird flaps his wings, rising up into the sky.

Nanita's new shoes are made of fine white pigskin. Her papa shows her how to rub the leather with her fingers until it is as thin and soft as rose petals. The shoes go *click, clack, clack* as Nanita proudly walks to her First Communion.

To celebrate, Nanita's papa announces a fiesta for everyone. Nanita decides to make flan. When her arm gets tired from whisking the eggs, she remembers what Señor Parrot told her and gives them ten more strokes.

At the fiesta the colonel says, "I salute this flan!"

The dancing teacher says, "Oh, this flan makes me want to twirl on my toes!"

The mayor says, "I declare this flan the official dessert of our village!"

The priest says, "This is heavenly flan!"

But best of all, as Nanita's papa takes a taste, he looks at her and the corners of his mouth turn up in a big smile.

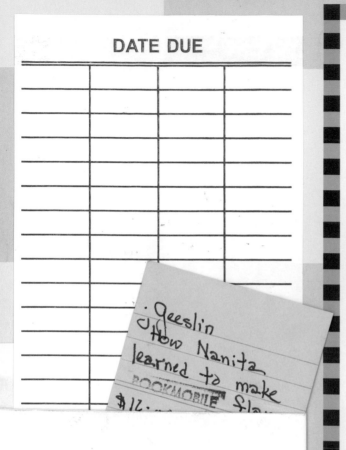

Nanita's flan

6 eggs

8 tablespoons plus 5 tablespoons sugar

4 teaspoons water

I cup fresh orange juice

Juice of half a lemon

I teaspoon grated orange rind

1/2 teaspoon grated lemon rind

Over low heat, stir constantly 8 tablespoons sugar and the water in a heavy pan or small skillet. When it darkens into caramel, divide and pour the syrup into six oven-safe cups.